Prologue

Three years ago — Hayes Ranch

Jaxon stood beneath the wide Texas sky, the kind of sky that made a man feel both infinite and small all at once.

But today, it only felt heavy.

The funeral was over. The crowd had left.
Only family lingered inside the house; voices hushed behind closed doors.

He stayed out here — alone — staring at the fresh grave under the old oak tree.

His father's name etched into the headstone.

William Hayes.
Loving husband. Devoted father. Builder of legacies.

Jaxon's jaw clenched as the weight of those last words pressed down harder than ever.

Builder of legacies.

And now it was his.

The land. The ranch. The empire his father built from nothing.

And all the expectations that came with it.

The sponsors. The press. The damn rodeo circuit that loved turning him into some larger-than-life cowboy.

They all expected him to fill those boots.
To never slip.
Never stumble.

To carry it perfectly.

But under the weight of grief, of responsibility, of the fear clawing silently behind his ribs—he didn't feel perfect.

He felt like a man barely holding it together.

Jaxon swallowed hard, his voice rough as he whispered into the wind.

"I won't screw this up, Dad. I swear."

The promise tasted like iron in his throat.

And even as the years passed, even as he threw himself into the rodeo circuit and sponsorship deals, even as the world called him reckless or arrogant or untouchable—
The guilt never left.

Because deep down, the one person he couldn't fool was himself.

Taming the Cowboy:

A Steamy Small-Town Enemies-to-Lovers Romance

Savannah Cross

Copyright

Present Day

He didn't know it yet, but soon someone would walk into his life — someone who wouldn't buy the show.

Someone who would see past the swagger and force him to face the truth he'd spent years avoiding.

Scarlett Monroe was coming to Willow Creek.

And nothing would ever be the same.

Contents

Chapter 1: The Scandal & The Arrival

Scarlett

It takes a lot to rattle me.

I've managed billionaires cheating on their wives, celebrities flashing body parts at award shows, and tech CEOs caught with offshore accounts. My job isn't to flinch — it's to fix.

But as I watch the video looping on my laptop, I can feel my perfectly steady pulse starting to tick faster.

The clip is grainy but unmistakable.

Jaxon Hayes — tall, broad-shouldered, jawline sharp enough to cut steel — is standing in the middle of a backwoods bar, grinning like a man who has zero regrets about what's happening.

Which is impressive, considering what's happening is a full-scale brawl.

Chairs flying. Glass breaking. Fists landing with satisfying thuds. The other guy — some local rancher from the town of Willow Creek — already flat on his back. Jaxon standing over him like he's just won the heavyweight title.

And then — the part that's now going viral — he turns to the camera, wipes a smear of blood from his lip, flashes a cocky grin, and says:

"Tell 'em I'll see 'em at the rodeo."

The video ends with the sound of a dozen smartphones clicking in unison.

I exhale slowly, closing the laptop.

I don't sigh. I don't pace. I certainly don't panic. Not my style. But the familiar tightness curls behind my ribcage. The same one that hits every time I realize the stakes just got higher.

A knock sounds on my office door.

I don't even look up. "Come in."

My assistant, Jessica, pokes her head in, eyes wide. "Adler wants you. Now."

Of course he does.

Adler & Co. is the most elite crisis management firm in Manhattan. And I'm its star closer.

I fix messes. I rebrand disasters. I control narratives.

I step into Adler's office, my heels clicking softly against the marble floors, calm and composed as always.

Adler barely glances up from his phone. "You've seen the video."

"Of course."

"The sponsors are losing their shit."

"They should be."

He finally looks up, leveling me with that dry, calculating stare he's perfected over the years. "I'm sending you to Texas."

That gets my attention.

"Texas?"

"Willow Creek. You'll be staying on the Hayes Ranch."

I blink. "You're serious."

"Dead serious."

"Adler—"

"You're the only one who can handle him."

I resist the urge to roll my eyes. "Adler, I specialize in politicians, corporate execs, billion-dollar brands—"

"And this is a billion-dollar brand." He cuts me off, voice clipped. "The Hayes family doesn't just own one of the biggest ranches in Texas — they own half the regional economy. They're land, cattle, energy, endorsements. And their golden boy is one viral punch away from losing every sponsor he's got."

I fold my arms, trying to keep my voice level. "The rodeo cowboy?"

"Exactly. Jaxon Hayes is more than a cowboy. He's the face of half our agriculture clients. The ranch wants him cleaned up before the National Finals in two months. If we lose him, we lose everything attached to him."

I glance back at the video thumbnail still flashing on my phone. Jaxon's grin practically dares me.

"He's not going to cooperate."

Adler leans back, smirking. "That's why I'm sending *you*."

Two days later, I'm on a flight to Texas, regretting every career decision that led me here.

The second the plane touches down, I know I'm not in Manhattan anymore.

The tiny regional airport smells like livestock and jet fuel. The sky is too big, the air too hot, and the people too friendly.

Waiting for me at baggage claim is a tall, lanky cowboy holding a cardboard sign that says *Monroe* in thick Sharpie.

"Miss Monroe?" he calls out.

"That's me."

He tips his hat with a polite smile. "I'm Wyatt. Jaxon's brother. He sent me to pick you up."

Of course he did.

I slide my sunglasses on, trying not to scowl. "Lead the way."

The drive from the airport to Willow Creek is… scenic.

Miles of open pasture. Cows. Horses. The occasional tractor crawling down a two-lane highway. I check my phone repeatedly out of habit, but reception is spotty at best.

Wyatt glances over with an easy smile. "Not exactly Fifth Avenue, huh?"

"Not quite."

He chuckles. "Jaxon warned us you'd be a tough one."

My jaw tics slightly. "Did he."

"Oh yeah. He's real curious about you."

"Curious how?"

"He's trying to guess how long you'll last."

I arch a brow. "Charming."

Wyatt laughs. "Don't take it personal. He likes poking the bear."

I stare out at the endless Texas horizon.

Let him poke.
I don't break.

When we finally pull through the gates of the Hayes Ranch, I realize just how large a problem I'm walking into.

The property is enormous — sprawling pastures, miles of white fencing, perfectly restored barns, and the main house standing like a Southern mansion straight out of a Nicholas Sparks adaptation.

Wyatt parks in front of the house, hops out, and grabs my luggage like a perfect gentleman.

"You hungry? Mama made a full spread."

"Very kind. But I'd like to meet with your brother first."

Wyatt nods. "I figured you might."

And that's when I hear it — the heavy, rhythmic thud of boots on polished wood.

Jaxon Hayes steps out onto the porch like he's walking into a movie scene.

And dammit if he doesn't fit the part perfectly.

Broad shoulders filling out a worn denim shirt, sleeves rolled up to his elbows. Faded jeans hugging long legs. Cowboy boots. Tan skin. A slow, lazy grin that practically drips confidence.

His eyes meet mine — piercing, amused.

"Well, well." His voice is smooth, low, and entirely too inviting. "They really did send New York's best."

Scarlett

Jaxon moves down the porch steps, his boots crunching against the gravel. His stride is slow, confident — deliberate. Like a predator circling something he knows he'll catch.

Me.

I keep my posture straight, my expression carefully neutral. I've dealt with bigger egos than his. Billionaires with god complexes. Movie stars with entourages. Elected officials who think rules don't apply to them.

Jaxon Hayes might be pretty, but I don't intimidate easy.

He stops a few feet in front of me, taking his sweet time looking me over. Not rude — just assessing.

"You don't look like you belong out here," he says finally, voice warm and just a little too amused.

"That's because I don't."

His grin widens. "You're honest. I like that."

"I'm not here to be liked."

"Good." His eyes flash with something sharper. "Because I don't need a babysitter."

I pull my sunglasses off and meet his gaze directly. "Actually, you need exactly that. You just don't realize it yet."

Wyatt lets out a soft whistle behind him, clearly enjoying the show.

I take a slow step forward, closing the distance between us until we're almost toe to toe.

"Here's how this works, Mr. Hayes," I say, keeping my voice cool and even. "Your sponsors are on the verge of pulling out. The media is circling like sharks. You're one viral video away from being blacklisted off every major circuit."

His grin doesn't falter. "And you're here to save me?"

"I'm here to control the narrative. But that only works if you cooperate."

He leans in slightly, dropping his voice. "What makes you think I will?"

"Because if you don't," I whisper back, "your career ends."

We stand like that for several long seconds — neither one of us blinking.

The heat between us hums, electric.

He straightens finally, laughing softly. "Damn. You really are as mean as they said."

"I'm not mean," I reply. "I'm effective."

He flashes that grin again — the one that makes every female rodeo fan in the country lose their minds. "Guess we'll see."

Jaxon

She's trouble.

The best kind.

Scarlett Monroe walks like she owns the place, even though everything about this ranch screams *not hers*. Perfectly pressed black slacks, fitted white blouse, city heels that are about to sink into my gravel driveway. That sharp little chin tilt. That don't-fuck-with-me tone.

I like poking at her because I can see it already — she's used to being in control.

But me?
I don't play by anyone's rules.

And watching her try to wrangle me might be the best entertainment I've had in months.

Scarlett

The guesthouse they assign me is beautiful — rustic chic with exposed beams, wide windows, and a wraparound porch that overlooks endless hills.

It's all very picturesque.

And completely wrong for me.

I'm used to skyline views, espresso bars, and 24-hour noise. This silence feels... suspicious.

I spend the afternoon setting up my work materials, reviewing Jaxon's entire media history — every interview, every headline, every sponsorship contract — and mapping out the full thirty-day rehabilitation plan.

By the time I finish, my eyes are dry and my jaw aches from clenching.

A knock sounds on the door.

I open it to find Jaxon standing there, two cold beers in hand.

"Thought I'd offer a peace offering," he says, holding one out.

I eye it. "I don't drink while I work."

"You're always working, aren't you?"

"That's why I'm good at what I do."

He smirks. "You should try relaxing sometime."

"I'll relax when your sponsors stop calling me in a panic."

He chuckles but doesn't leave. "Can I come in?"

"Only if you're ready to talk business."

He steps inside, looking around the cozy living room like he's assessing my battlefield.

"All right, boss lady," he says, settling into one of the oversized leather chairs. "Let's hear it."

I grab my tablet, flipping it around to show him the color-coded schedule. "Media training starts tomorrow. We have public appearances lined up — charity events, interviews, sponsor dinners. You'll follow my lead at all times. No freelancing. No surprises."

He raises a brow. "You always plan every second of your life?"

"Yes."

"That sounds exhausting."

"It's effective."

"You said that already."

"Because it's true."

He laughs softly, shaking his head. "God help me."

"Help yourself, Mr. Hayes. Cooperate, and this all goes away."

"And if I don't?"

I level him with a look. "If you don't, I'll bury you so fast you'll think this ranch was your own grave."

His eyes spark with something dangerous — not anger.

Admiration.

"You're fun."

"I'm not here to be fun."

"Too late," he says, standing slowly. "You are."

He heads for the door, but not before glancing back one more time.

"Sweet dreams, city girl."

I slam the door behind him a little harder than necessary.

And curse myself for the tiny flutter in my stomach that absolutely should not be there.

Scarlett

By morning, the ranch is buzzing.

The smell of fresh hay and coffee floats through the air as I step onto the porch, tablet in hand, ready to wrangle my client into his first media training session.

I've run thousands of these.

Crisis PR 101: Build the talking points. Practice the answers. Train the delivery. Control the narrative.

What I don't usually have to deal with is a subject like Jaxon Hayes.

I find him by the stables, brushing down one of his horses like there's not a single care in the world.

"Good morning, Miss Monroe," he drawls without looking up.

"Mr. Hayes."

He finishes with the horse and finally turns, that lazy grin locked and loaded. "Ready to fix me?"

"Let's start with you sitting down and shutting up."

He laughs. "Bossy."

"Efficient." I glance around. "We're doing this here."

His brows lift. "Out in the open?"

"Yes. The more comfortable you are in your normal environment, the easier it'll be to integrate the messaging."

He studies me for a moment. "You like control, don't you?"

"I like results."

"Same thing."

I take a seat on the low fence rail and click my tablet on. "We'll start with basic messaging. Repeat after me: 'I take full responsibility for my actions and am committed to earning back the trust of my sponsors, fans, and community.'"

He snorts. "Hell of a mouthful."

"Say it."

He raises both hands in mock surrender. "All right, all right." He clears his throat dramatically. "'I take full responsibility for my... poor decision-making, and will try real hard not to punch any more assholes.'"

I don't react.

He grins wider. "That was close, right?"

"Again."

He sighs heavily, then repeats it properly this time.

Almost.

I lean forward. "Tone matters. You sound like you're reading a hostage note."

"Maybe I am."

I fix him with a steady look. "You want sponsors? You want to keep your rodeo contracts? Then take this seriously."

He steps closer, arms folding across his broad chest. "And what if I don't give a damn about sponsors?"

I arch a brow. "Do you give a damn about this ranch? Your family? The dozens of people whose jobs depend on the deals your name secures?"

His jaw tenses. For the first time, the teasing fades.

Bullseye.

"You think I don't care about my family?" he asks softly, voice lower now.

"I think you let your pride make very expensive decisions."

His gaze sharpens, the flirt gone, replaced by something heavier.

We stand in that weight for a long moment.

Finally, he exhales, running a hand through his hair. "You don't pull punches."

"No."

"And you don't scare easy."

"No."

His mouth twitches like he's fighting a smile. "That makes you dangerous."

I stare back. "And that makes you my job."

The heat between us thickens like heavy summer air. The kind that warns of a storm coming.

But before anything else can be said, a voice calls out behind us.

"Scarlett!" Sadie — Jaxon's sister-in-law — waves from across the yard, wearing cut-off shorts and a bright smile. "Come join us for breakfast before he scares you off completely!"

"I don't scare her," Jaxon says under his breath.

"Not yet," I mutter.

Breakfast at the Ranch

I follow Sadie into the massive farmhouse kitchen where Mama Hayes is already pouring fresh coffee and piling biscuits high onto warm plates.

"Sit, honey," Mama says cheerfully, patting the chair next to hers. "Don't let my boys work you too hard."

I offer a polite smile. "Thank you. The hospitality is lovely."

Sadie leans in with a wink. "You're braver than most. Jaxon usually scares the fancy ones off by day two."

"Is that so?"

"Oh, yeah." She nods. "The last PR rep left crying."

I glance sideways at Jaxon as he drops into his chair across from me. He's listening to every word, clearly enjoying this.

"Don't listen to them," he says. "I'm delightful."

"Hmm," I hum, sipping my coffee. "Not the word I'd use."

The whole table laughs.

I let the banter roll as I mentally take stock of the situation.

The family likes me.

The staff respects me.

The media schedule is built.

The sponsors are watching.

And Jaxon Hayes?

He's still testing me.

But he's going to learn very quickly —

No one breaks me.

Especially not a cocky cowboy with dangerous blue eyes and a grin that belongs on a billboard.

Chapter 2: The First Clash

Scarlett

Jaxon Hayes is officially my most difficult client.

And that includes the tech CEO who accidentally live-streamed his own bachelor party.

By mid-morning, I've already had to stop him from blowing off a video interview, redirect him twice during a sponsor call, and remind him — very firmly — that "winging it" is not a viable PR strategy.

He's impossible.

And yet somehow, dangerously charming while doing it.

We're standing under the bright Texas sun now, preparing for our first major PR shoot — a carefully staged "community outreach" event with one of the local children's charities.

A photographer circles us, snapping candids as Jaxon signs autographs, lifts kids onto horses, and flashes that smile that drives his fanbase crazy.

And I hate to admit it — he's good at this part. When he wants to be.

The sponsors will eat these images alive.

I stay back, managing the media crew, keeping everything on schedule, when I feel him slide in next to me during a break.

"Not bad, huh?" he asks, his voice low and playful.

"You're still on probation."

He grins. "Didn't see you scolding me just now."

"Because you finally managed to follow directions."

"That almost sounded like a compliment."

"Don't get used to it."

He studies me for a beat, eyes narrowed like he's trying to solve a puzzle. "You're harder to rattle than I thought."

"Because I know your type."

"My type?"

"Cocky. Charming. Reckless. Used to women falling all over you."

"Is that what you think?"

"It's what I know."

He steps closer, his voice dipping lower. "You sure you've got me all figured out already?"

I don't flinch, but my pulse ticks faster.

"You're not that complicated."

"And yet you're staring at my mouth right now."

I snap my gaze up, giving him my iciest glare. "You're imagining things."

He smiles, slow and easy. "No, I'm not."

The photographer calls him back to the horses, and just like that, he strolls off like nothing happened.

I exhale sharply, pressing my tablet tighter against my chest.

He's baiting me.

And worse — it's starting to work.

Jaxon

Scarlett Monroe is wound tight.

Perfect posture. Perfect lipstick. Perfect control.

And God help me, I want to see what she looks like when she finally cracks.

She watches me like I'm a bomb she has to keep defused.

But what she doesn't know is — part of me wants to explode.

Every time she steps close with that sharp little voice and those endless legs in those city heels, it makes me want to do very unprofessional things.

Things that don't belong on any PR schedule.

Later — The First Official Clash

We're back at the ranch after the charity event, sitting at the long dining table with his family for another meal that feels half like hospitality, half like interrogation.

"So, Scarlett," Wyatt says with a teasing grin, "how's our boy doing? You fixing him yet?"

I glance at Jaxon across the table. "We're making progress."

"He's a handful," Sadie adds. "Always has been."

Jaxon just grins, leaning back in his chair. "You're all acting like I'm a lost cause."

"You were," Beau mutters.

I keep my voice light but firm. "He's salvageable."

Jaxon leans forward, voice low and teasing. "Is that your professional opinion?"

"It's my miracle-worker opinion."

His grin turns slow, dangerous. "And how long do miracles usually take?"

"As long as it takes for you to stop acting like a child."

The whole table falls silent for a beat.

Then Mama Hayes lets out a soft laugh. "Well, I like her."

Everyone laughs — even Jaxon.

But under the table, I feel his knee brush lightly against mine.

A deliberate touch.

Testing.

I shift away subtly, ignoring the heat rising in my cheeks.

I cannot afford to play this game.

After Dinner — The Real Push

As I retreat toward the guesthouse, I hear his voice behind me.

"Scarlett."

I stop, turning slowly.

Jaxon steps closer, his voice softer now, less playful.

"You really think I'm reckless?"

"I think you're afraid."

That gives him pause.

"Afraid of what?"

"Of failing."

He watches me carefully, the teasing gone. "That's not your job to figure out."

"No, but it's my job to make sure you stop giving everyone else reasons to doubt you."

I turn to go, but he catches my wrist — gentle, not forceful.

The contact sparks through me like static.

"You ever let anyone see behind all that armor of yours?" he asks softly.

I stare up at him, breath caught.

"Don't push your luck, Mr. Hayes."

He smiles — but it's softer this time. "That's what I'm good at."

Scarlett

The problem with small towns?

There's no such thing as privacy.

The next morning, I barely make it to Lulu's Café — the only decent coffee spot within twenty miles — before I'm met with the familiar sound of whispering.

"That's her."
"The city girl with Jaxon."
"Pretty, but she won't last."

I ignore them.

My job isn't to make friends. It's to manage public perception. The whispers come with the territory.

Still, the way they openly stare as I walk to the counter is enough to make even my thick skin prickle.

Sadie waves me over from a corner booth. "You're already famous, honey."

I sigh, sliding into the seat across from her. "Famous or infamous?"

"In this town?" She grins. "Same thing."

I accept the coffee she pushes toward me, grateful for at least one ally here. "I thought we were calming the rumors."

Sadie's smile softens. "You're doing great, honestly. But people around here get excited about any new headline."

"Especially romantic ones," I mutter.

Her eyes sparkle. "You two do make quite the pair."

"We are not a pair."

"Sure."

I glare, but she's unfazed.

"You know," she continues, leaning in conspiratorially, "he hasn't looked at anyone like this since... well, ever."

I stiffen. "Sadie—"

"I'm just saying." She lifts her hands innocently. "The way he watches you? It's not professional."

I take a long sip of coffee, letting the warmth fill my chest. "We have rules."

"Mm-hmm. And how long do you plan to pretend those rules are working?"

Before I can answer, my phone buzzes sharply.

Adler:

Sponsorship board check-in this afternoon. Make sure Jaxon's polished.

Back to work.

Back to control.

I stand. "I should get back."

Sadie watches me with that knowing smile as I leave.

And even as I step out into the warm Texas sun, her words follow me like a shadow.

The way he watches you.

Jaxon

The funny thing is — Sadie's not wrong.

Scarlett thinks she's hiding how she feels. But I see it.

Every time I step a little too close.
Every time my hand brushes hers.
Every time she loses her breath for half a second before snapping back into control.

She's not as untouchable as she wants to be.

And that?

That makes this game way too damn tempting.

The Afternoon Sponsor Call — First Real Crack

We sit side by side at the big oak table in the main house, video conference glowing on my laptop screen.

Adler appears, flanked by two stone-faced sponsor reps from the primary beef distributor that pays for half my damn rodeo career.

Scarlett takes the lead flawlessly, laying out our progress like the perfect crisis handler she is.

"Our engagement strategy has stabilized public sentiment," she explains smoothly. "The recent charity event was covered favorably by three national outlets. Sponsorship risk has dropped significantly."

One of the reps nods. "That's reassuring. But we still need to be confident Jaxon understands the gravity of his behavior."

All eyes turn to me.

Here we go.

Scarlett gives me the smallest, almost imperceptible nod — a cue we practiced.

I clear my throat, forcing my tone steady.

"I take full responsibility for my mistakes," I say, repeating the line we drilled. "I've let emotions get the better of me, but I'm committed to rebuilding trust — both professionally and personally."

A beat of silence.

Adler arches a brow, surprised.

Scarlett's smile barely shifts, but I feel the pride radiating off her.

The sponsors nod.

The call ends without incident.

The second the screen goes dark, Scarlett exhales, finally relaxing.

"That," she says softly, "was perfect."

"Wasn't so hard."

She gives me a look. "Don't ruin it."

I can't help but smile. "You were worried."

"I'm always worried."

I lean back in my chair, letting my gaze slide over her. "You don't need to be."

Her eyes meet mine. "That's my job."

"No," I say, voice lower now. "Your job is to protect my image. But lately? Feels like you're protecting me."

Her breath catches.

She opens her mouth, but no words come out.

The silence thickens between us — not tense.

Heavy.
Loaded.
Dangerous.

Finally, she stands, pulling herself together with that sharp little snap I've come to recognize.

"Good work today, Jaxon."

I watch her leave, that tight sway of her hips impossible to ignore.

And I know:

We're both losing this battle.

Scarlett

By the time I reach my guesthouse, my hands are shaking.

Because he's right.

Somewhere along the way, this stopped being about the sponsors.

And started being about *him*.

Chapter 3: Small Town & Growing Tension

Scarlett

I've been in small towns before.

But Willow Creek?
Willow Creek operates like a single living organism.

Everyone knows everything.
And everyone loves to *talk*.

By the end of the week, half the town seems to have adopted me like some sort of exotic zoo exhibit.

The new rumor mill highlight?

That Jaxon and I are secretly dating.

The first time I hear it whispered, I almost laugh. The second time, I stiffen. By the third time, I start wondering if maybe I'm losing control of this entire operation.

Because the worst part is — the cameras might be getting the wrong idea, but they're not entirely wrong.

The attraction is getting harder to manage.

Today's PR Disaster in the Making: The Charity Rodeo Auction

The event is packed — local vendors, media cameras, sponsors, and plenty of curious residents angling for a glimpse of Willow Creek's most notorious bad boy and his *mysterious city woman.*

I walk beside Jaxon, clipboard in hand, managing interviews and sponsor greetings like clockwork.

His hand drifts to the small of my back more than once.

Professional.
Casual.
Believable.

Except every time his fingers brush my waist, it feels less like an act and more like a spark thrown onto dry grass.

"Relax," he murmurs near my ear as we approach another group of cameras. "You look like you're about to bolt."

"Because I am."

He smiles lazily. "You're doing great, city girl."

"I'm not your girlfriend, Jaxon."

"Tell that to everyone here." He flashes a grin as the flashbulbs pop around us. "They're eating this up."

I clench my jaw, holding my professional smile as the reporter steps closer.

"Scarlett, is it true you and Jaxon are officially dating?" she asks sweetly.

Before I can shut it down, Jaxon answers.

"We're just taking things slow," he says with a wink. "But I'm hoping she'll stick around."

The cameras erupt in excited murmurs.

I shoot him a deadly glare.

He shrugs innocently. "You want them to believe the redemption story, don't you?"

Jaxon

She's going to murder me.

But damn if she doesn't look even hotter when she's mad.

The way she grits her teeth under that fake smile?
The way her eyes narrow like she's two seconds from snapping?
Perfect.

I shouldn't enjoy poking her like this.

But I do.

Because beneath all that control? She wants me just as bad as I want her.

The Ex Appears

We barely survive the media blitz before the next storm hits.

Lila.

Her voice cuts through the crowd like a blade dipped in honey.

"Well, well. If it isn't my favorite cowboy."

We both turn as she saunters toward us in tight jeans, tall boots, and a smile sharp enough to draw blood.

Her eyes flick over me before landing squarely on Scarlett.

"And you must be the new... what's the word?" She smiles innocently. "Handler?"

Scarlett doesn't flinch. "Publicist."

"Mmm." Lila's eyes sparkle. "That's adorable."

I step between them slightly. "Lila, we're busy."

"Oh, don't mind me," she purrs. "Just wanted to say hi."

Her gaze locks onto Scarlett again. "How's ranch life treating you, sugar?"

Scarlett's voice stays cool. "I adapt quickly."

Lila laughs lightly. "We'll see."

The tension between them hums like a live wire.

Scarlett doesn't break eye contact. "Yes. We will."

Lila finally retreats with a little smirk, leaving a trail of sticky sweetness behind her.

I glance at Scarlett once she's gone. "Handled that like a pro."

She exhales sharply. "Is she going to be a problem?"

I consider. "Depends."

"On what?"

"On whether or not she realizes she's already lost."

Her breath hitches slightly before she covers it with a sharp pivot. "Let's get back to work."

But as we walk away, I see her steal a glance at me.

And for the first time, I wonder who exactly is chasing who anymore.

Scarlett

If there's one thing worse than being trapped in a PR disaster, it's being trapped in a PR disaster inside a house full of matchmakers.

By the time we get back to the ranch after the charity event, Mama Hayes has somehow orchestrated what she calls a "family night."

Which means I'm now sitting at their massive farmhouse table, surrounded by the entire Hayes clan, as they pretend this isn't an interrogation disguised as dinner.

Jaxon's brothers, Wyatt and Beau, keep trading smug glances. Sadie keeps giving me little nudges every time Jaxon so much as looks my way.
And Mama Hayes is watching me like she's sizing me up for a wedding dress.

"I hope you like peach cobbler," Mama says sweetly, sliding a warm dish in front of me.

"I love it," I lie.

Because how do you tell the matriarch of the ranch that you have zero appetite when her son keeps brushing his leg against yours under the table?

"You're adjusting well," Mama adds. "Jaxon can be a bit...
stubborn."

"Just a bit," Sadie mutters.

Jaxon laughs easily. "Come on, y'all. I'm a delight."

I shoot him a look. "Delightful isn't the word I'd use."

Wyatt leans in with a grin. "Scarlett, how long are you staying
again?"

"As long as it takes," I say smoothly, "to make sure Jaxon
stays out of trouble."

The table laughs.

But Jaxon?
He's watching me. Closely.

And beneath the teasing, I see it — that flicker of something
dangerous and real.

Attraction isn't the problem.

Wanting isn't the problem.

It's everything else.

Later — The Storm Rolls In

That night, the Texas sky opens up.

The rain starts as a soft patter, but quickly grows into a full-blown storm. Wind howls across the open fields, rattling the old window frames of the guesthouse.

The lights flicker once, twice, then go out.

Perfect.

I fumble for my flashlight, cursing softly.

A knock at the door nearly makes me jump.

I pull it open to find Jaxon standing there, soaked from the rain, his hat dripping.

"Power's out across the property," he says. "Figured you might not want to sit alone in the dark."

I hesitate.

"Strictly professional, of course," he adds with a grin.

I roll my eyes but step aside. "Come in."

Forced Proximity

The guesthouse feels smaller with him inside it.

We sit on the couch, wrapped in the soft glow of a few battery-powered lanterns, the rain drumming steady against the roof.

For several long minutes, we sit in silence.

And somehow, it's worse than talking.

Finally, Jaxon shifts slightly, his voice softer than I've heard it all week.

"You don't like storms, do you?"

I glance at him. "I don't like losing control."

"That's what this is about for you."

"This job is about control," I reply. "Predictability. Managing variables."

He watches me closely. "And I'm not predictable."

"No."

"Does that scare you?"

I don't answer.

Because it does.

Not because he's unpredictable professionally — but because he's unpredictable *personally*.

He leans in a little closer, lowering his voice even more. "I can make it real simple, Scarlett."

"How's that?"

"You don't have to control everything tonight."

My breath hitches.

The warmth of him inches away is electric. His scent — rain, leather, something wholly *him* — wraps around me, making my brain short-circuit.

His hand brushes my knee lightly.

Not demanding.
Not urgent.
Just a question, wordless.

My heart slams against my ribcage.

I should pull back.

I should say something sharp, deflect, redirect — anything.

But I don't.

I stay frozen.

He leans in further, his lips hovering dangerously close to mine.

"We don't have to pretend right now," he whispers.

The air between us is thick, humming.

I tip forward — barely, instinctively — and that's when a loud crack of thunder splits the sky, shaking the entire house.

We both jump slightly, breaking the spell.

Jaxon chuckles softly, pulling back an inch. "Texas storms ruin everything."

I exhale shakily, trying to find my voice. "Maybe that was for the best."

He watches me a beat longer, the heat still simmering behind his eyes.

"Maybe," he agrees quietly.

But we both know — it's only a matter of time before we stop pretending.

Scarlett

I sit alone after he leaves, the rain pounding outside, my pulse refusing to settle.

Because he's right.

The pretending is getting harder.

And the next time he leans in like that, I don't know if I'll stop him.

Chapter 4: The Ex Returns & Jealousy

Scarlett

I'm starting to understand something about Willow Creek:

The gossip isn't a side effect.
It's the heartbeat.

And today, that heartbeat is racing.

Because Lila Matthews is back.

The news reaches me before I even see her.

The whispers buzz everywhere — at the café, the grocery store, even at the gas station when I stopped for coffee. Every overly-friendly smile from the locals carries a subtext I can feel like static in the air.

The ex is back.

And judging by the saccharine tone of everyone's voices, Lila's return isn't casual.

She's here to reclaim something.

Or rather... someone.

The Setup

The sponsors scheduled a press luncheon — one of our carefully staged public events to continue rehabilitating Jaxon's image. Clean, controlled, simple.

At least, it was supposed to be.

I arrive early, scanning the tables, briefing the staff, mentally reviewing the talking points we drilled into Jaxon.

He arrives a few minutes later, looking infuriatingly perfect in a crisp button-down, dark jeans, and that damn cocky grin.

"Don't worry, boss lady," he says as he joins me. "I'll behave."

"You better."

He leans closer, dropping his voice. "You sure you're not starting to enjoy bossing me around?"

I glare. "Focus."

He chuckles. "Focused."

And for the first few minutes, everything goes smoothly.

Until she arrives.

The Ex Makes Her Move

Lila walks in like she owns the room.

Blonde waves perfectly styled. Slim, designer jeans that probably cost more than most people's rent. Boots that click sharply on the polished floor as she strides toward us, her smile wide and predatory.

Jaxon stiffens immediately beside me.

"Well, well," Lila drawls, stopping right in front of us. "Look who cleaned up nicely."

"Lila," Jaxon says, polite but flat.

Her eyes shift to me, taking me in with one slow, calculating sweep.

"And you must be Scarlett."

I extend my hand with a cool smile. "Scarlett Monroe."

She takes it briefly. "Publicist, right?"

"Yes."

"So, you're the one making sure my cowboy here stays out of trouble."

"I do my best," I say smoothly.

Her eyes glint. "He does like trouble, doesn't he?"

The dig is subtle, but sharp.

I keep my face neutral. "Only when unsupervised."

Her smile falters — just slightly.

But Jaxon steps in before I can say more. "We've got interviews to prep for, Lila."

She hums softly. "Of course. I wouldn't want to interrupt."

Her gaze flickers back to me one last time, sweet and sharp. "Good luck, Scarlett. Ranch life's not for everyone."

I hold her stare evenly. "Neither is losing."

Lila's smile tightens. She gives Jaxon a final once-over before sauntering away.

Jaxon

Scarlett handled that like a goddamn queen.

Cool.
Controlled.
Deadly sharp.

And yet, even as she keeps her perfect PR mask locked in place, I can see the crack beneath it.

The way her shoulders stiffened.

The brief flicker of fire in her eyes.

She won't admit it — but Lila got under her skin.

And I'd be lying if I said I didn't like seeing her flustered for once.

But more than that?

I want her to know she never needs to compete.
Because there's no comparison.

Scarlett

The luncheon wraps successfully — at least on paper.

The sponsors leave happy. The press gets their photo ops. The headlines tomorrow will continue feeding the redemption narrative.

But as I climb into Jaxon's truck for the ride back to the ranch, my stomach is still twisting.

I hate that she got to me.

I hate that she saw exactly how to needle me.

And most of all, I hate that part of me *cares*.

Jaxon starts driving, quiet for a few minutes before finally glancing at me.

"She's not a problem," he says softly.

I keep my gaze forward. "She seems eager to be."

"She doesn't matter."

I let out a dry laugh. "You dated her."

"I also broke up with her."

"She obviously didn't get the memo."

He watches me for a beat longer before turning his eyes back to the road.

"I don't want her, Scarlett," he says quietly. "I want you."

The words land like a punch to the chest.

Hot.
Simple.
Undeniably real.

I swallow hard, my pulse racing. "This isn't about what you want."

"No?" His voice lowers. "Because it sure as hell feels like it is."

I don't answer.

Because we both know I'm already standing dangerously close to the edge.

Scarlett

By the time we get back to the ranch, I'm wound so tight my muscles ache.

I head straight to the guesthouse, desperate for space, but of course, that's not how small-town ranch life works.

Not when everyone thinks you're already part of the family.

Family Meddling: Round Two

I barely make it five steps before Sadie intercepts me on the porch.

"Scarlett! Perfect timing. Mama's baking, and we're planning the fall festival."

"I really should—"

"Nope." She loops her arm through mine and pulls me inside like I don't have a choice.

I'm deposited at the kitchen table again, surrounded by smiling faces.

Mama slides a fresh plate of cookies toward me. "Scarlett, dear, I hope you're still planning to stay a while longer."

"I... well—"

"Oh, give her a break, Mama," Wyatt grins. "She's got her hands full with our disaster of a brother."

Beau smirks. "He's been weirdly well-behaved, actually."

"That's what love does to a man," Sadie adds with a pointed glance my way.

I nearly choke on my cookie.

"It's not love," I say quickly. "It's work."

"Mm-hmm," Mama says softly, that knowing, patient smile spreading across her face.

Before I can escape, Jaxon strolls in behind me, towel slung over one shoulder, fresh from the barn.

He doesn't say a word — just leans casually against the doorframe and watches.

Like he knows exactly how uncomfortable I am.

And exactly how much I'm starting to like it.

Later That Night — The Breaking Point

The storm breaks again after midnight.

A late summer rain rolls across the fields, heavy and warm. I lie in bed staring at the ceiling, replaying the day like a reel of mistakes.

The way Lila's words dug under my skin.

The way Jaxon's eyes locked on mine in the truck.

The way my own traitorous heart keeps pounding every time he gets too close.

I give up trying to sleep and wander out onto the porch.

The rain has slowed to a light mist, the night air thick and soft.

And of course, he's there.

Leaning against the porch rail, arms folded, like he's been waiting for me.

"Can't sleep?" he asks softly.

"No."

He nods, as if he understands completely. "Me neither."

We stand there for a few moments, listening to the rain patter against the tin roof.

Then, softly, he says, "You handled Lila better than I ever did."

I exhale a humorless laugh. "She was trying to get to me."

"She succeeded."

My head snaps toward him, but he isn't smirking. He's watching me carefully.

"It bothers you," he continues. "The idea of me being with her."

I clench my jaw. "It bothers me when anyone tries to undermine my work."

"That's not what I'm talking about, and you know it."

The air thickens between us again.

"You're crossing the line," I whisper.

His voice drops low. "I think we crossed it a long time ago."

He steps closer, every inch of him radiating heat.

I don't back away.

"I don't want to make this harder than it already is," I say, my voice shaky.

"Then stop pretending you don't want me."

I open my mouth — to argue, to deny, to say *anything* — but nothing comes out.

Because he's right.

And when his hand lifts to tuck a damp strand of hair behind my ear, my body betrays me completely.

I lean into his touch.

His thumb grazes my cheek, his breath warm against my skin.

"Scarlett," he whispers, his voice rough, "tell me to stop."

I can't.

I don't.

His lips brush mine — not fully kissing, just hovering, teasing, daring me to close the gap.

I hover there, my breath catching, every nerve in my body screaming for him.

And then—

The door creaks behind us.

We spring apart like guilty teenagers as Mama steps out onto the porch, squinting into the dark.

"Oh!" she gasps softly. "Didn't mean to interrupt."

I take a step back, desperately trying to steady my breath. "It's fine. I was just getting some air."

Mama smiles gently, her eyes sparkling like she knows exactly what she walked in on.

"Don't let me stop you two," she says sweetly, before disappearing back inside.

The moment is broken.

But the damage is done.

The line we've been trying to walk is practically gone now.

It's only a matter of time before we fall.

Scarlett

I lie awake the rest of the night, my pulse refusing to calm.

Because what scares me most isn't how close we came to kissing.

It's how badly I wanted to.

Chapter 5: Emotional Vulnerabilities Surface

Scarlett

I've built my career on being able to read people.

Their patterns. Their tells.
The way their voices shift when they're lying.
The way their bodies tense when they're hiding something.

But Jaxon Hayes is a different kind of puzzle.

Because sometimes, he's so open it's disarming.
And sometimes, he's so closed off I feel like I'm talking to brick.

And lately, I've started to realize — his cockiness isn't armor.

It's protection.

The morning after our almost-kiss, I walk into the main house with my tablet, expecting him to be halfway through breakfast, charming his family as usual.

Instead, the kitchen is empty.

Sadie's not here. Wyatt's truck is gone. Even Mama Hayes is missing.

But Jaxon?

He's out by the barn, alone, working a young horse in the round pen.

His movements are steady, focused, almost meditative. The horse circles him in wide, even loops — snorting, testing, but ultimately submitting to his calm control.

He doesn't notice me watching him at first.

Or maybe he does.

Either way, I'm hesitant to interrupt.

There's something raw about him this morning — stripped back. No grin. No teasing. Just... quiet.

Finally, he glances over, giving me a faint nod.

"You're up early," he says, voice low.

"I'm always up early."

"Control freak," he teases lightly, but his heart isn't fully in it today.

I step up to the fence rail, watching him work.

"You okay?"

He keeps his eyes on the horse. "I'm fine."

Liar.

Jaxon

The thing about growing up on a ranch is — you learn young how to bottle things up.

When something breaks, you fix it.
When something dies, you bury it.
When something scares you, you pretend it doesn't.

And lately?
Scarlett scares the hell out of me.

Not because she's sharp. Or bossy.
But because she makes me want things I told myself years ago I didn't get to want anymore.

Things like... *more.*

"You don't have to do this alone, you know," Scarlett says softly from behind me.

I keep working the horse, keeping my voice steady. "Do what?"

"Carry it all."

I glance at her now, catching that little crease between her brows that only shows when she's worried.

"Ranch life's like this, Scarlett. You keep moving. You carry what you need to."

"Until you drop it."

I smile faintly. "You think I'm about to drop?"

"I think you've been carrying too much for too long."

I stop the horse, finally turning to face her fully.

"You really think you've figured me out already, huh?"

She shrugs, trying to stay professional but failing. "I'm observant."

"No." I step closer, lowering my voice. "You're getting personal."

Her breath catches, but she holds her ground.

"That's dangerous," she whispers.

"For who?"

She swallows hard. "Both of us."

Scarlett

I knew coming here would be complicated.

But I didn't expect this.

Didn't expect him.

The way he looks at me — like he sees right through all my carefully built walls. Like I'm not just his publicist, but something... more.

And the worst part?

Part of me wants to be.

Even though I shouldn't.

Especially because I shouldn't.

Later — A Rare Moment of Honesty

That afternoon, we sit together on the wide porch swing after another round of sponsor calls and media training sessions.

The sun is setting, casting the whole ranch in warm gold.

He's quiet again.

I glance at him. "You want to talk about what's really bothering you?"

He lets out a soft breath, rubbing his jaw.

"You want honesty?"

"Yes."

He glances at me, his eyes dark and open in a way that makes my chest tighten.

"My dad built this place from nothing. Bought his first parcel of land when he was nineteen. Spent decades growing it. Built a business big enough to keep half this town working."

I stay silent, letting him go at his own pace.

"When I was a kid, I thought he was indestructible. He made everything look easy."

His voice softens. "Then one winter, he got sick. Quick. And everything stopped feeling easy."

My chest aches as he talks, his voice rough around the edges.

"I promised him I'd keep the ranch going. Take care of Mama. Take care of everyone."

He swallows. "And every time I screw up — like that bar fight — I feel like I'm failing him. Failing them."

I reach over without thinking, placing my hand lightly over his.

"You're not failing, Jaxon."

He looks at our hands. "Some days it feels like I am."

I squeeze his hand gently. "You're human. You're allowed to struggle."

He finally looks up at me, his eyes searching mine.

"Most people only see the headlines, Scarlett. The cocky rodeo cowboy. The bad boy. But you? You see more."

I swallow, my voice thin. "That's what scares me."

He tilts his head. "Why?"

"Because I don't know how to turn that off."

Scarlett

I didn't come here to feel anything.

I came here to fix him.
To fix this.

But somewhere between the sponsorship contracts, the forced proximity, and the late-night porch talks, my walls have started to crumble.

And I don't know how to stop it.

The silence stretches between us on the swing, but this time it feels comfortable. Intimate.

I take a deep breath.

"My mom used to say I was too much."

Jaxon glances at me, surprised. "You?"

I nod, forcing a small smile. "I always had big ideas. Big plans. Big ambitions. I wanted more than what our tiny town offered, and people didn't like that. Especially not for a girl."

I pause, feeling the old sting of it again.

"They called me arrogant. Cold. Unlikable."

Jaxon's brow furrows. "They were idiots."

I laugh softly. "Small towns have rules. I broke them. So I left. I ran to New York and built my walls high."

"And never looked back?"

I hesitate.

"Looking back means remembering how small I felt there. How much it hurt to be different."

He studies me for a moment, his gaze gentle.

"You're not too much, Scarlett," he says softly. "You're exactly enough."

The words nearly unravel me.

Because no one's ever said that before.

I blink hard, my throat tightening. "You don't know me well enough to say that."

"I know enough."

He shifts closer now, his thigh brushing mine.

His voice lowers. "You think you're protecting yourself by staying in control. But I see you trying to breathe underneath all that pressure."

My breath hitches.

Because he's right.

He sees too much.

And I'm terrified of how much I want him to keep seeing.

The Proposal

The knock on the door interrupts us just as the air grows too heavy.

Sadie pops her head out onto the porch. "Hey, sorry — sponsors called. Minor issue."

I exhale, forcing myself back into professional mode. "On it."

She hesitates. "Also… um, quick heads-up? The local news station wants to do a feature. Community interest angle."

"Fine."

"They want to cover you two as a couple."

I freeze. "What?"

"Not officially. Just... the image sells. The public loves it. The redemption narrative is playing well."

Jaxon arches a brow. "You hear that? We're selling well."

I glare at him. "This isn't funny."

But Sadie's already grinning. "Honestly? Might be smart to lean into it a little. Public opinion loves a love story."

Jaxon smirks, leaning into me. "See? Everybody wins."

I turn back to Sadie. "We'll discuss it."

Sadie winks and disappears back inside.

The second she's gone, I whirl on Jaxon. "Absolutely not."

"Why not?" he asks, too casual.

"Because fake relationships complicate everything."

"We're already pretending, Scarlett."

"Not like that."

"Isn't that what you're doing every time you tell the sponsors we're fine?"

I open my mouth, but he cuts me off, his voice dropping lower.

"This wouldn't be entirely fake," he says softly.

The heat between us spikes again.

"You want to pretend," I whisper, pulse racing. "But we both know we're already playing with fire."

"I like fire," he murmurs.

I swallow hard, every part of me screaming *danger.*

And yet... my professional brain starts calculating.

From a PR standpoint?
It would work.

It would stabilize the sponsors.
It would give the media something positive to cling to.
It would extend his redemption arc.

It would give me more time.

More time with him.

That thought makes my chest ache.

"Rules," I say finally. "Strict ones."

His grin is slow, dangerous. "Whatever you say, boss."

The Line Blurs

The next morning, we hold our first staged "couple" shoot for the media.

The local photographer directs us to sit close on the ranch fence, the golden sunrise casting perfect light across the open fields.

"Just relax," the photographer says cheerfully. "Lean into each other. Act natural."

Jaxon's hand slides easily around my waist, pulling me against his side.

His breath is warm against my ear. "See? Natural."

My pulse skyrockets.

We smile for the camera.

The perfect picture.

The perfect lie.

And the most terrifying thing is — part of me doesn't want it to be fake anymore.

Scarlett

I was never supposed to fall for my clients.

And I sure as hell wasn't supposed to fall for *him*.

But as his hand lingers a little too long on my waist after the cameras stop flashing, I know:

I'm already falling.

And I'm not sure I want to stop.

Chapter 6: Fake Dating Fully Activated

Scarlett

There's nothing more dangerous than a lie that starts to feel good.

And this one?
This one feels too good.

The local press eats it up.

The "new relationship" storyline spreads like wildfire — glowing headlines, adorable photos, soft-focus shots of Jaxon and me "cuddling" on hay bales, smiling for the cameras like we've been married for years.

The sponsors are ecstatic.
The town is delighted.
The redemption arc is working better than I ever could have scripted.

And that should comfort me.

But every time his hand slides around my waist in public, I feel my pulse spike.

Because it doesn't feel like acting.

Not anymore.

The Breakfast Ambush

"You know, honey, you could just move into the big house," Mama says sweetly over breakfast one morning.

I nearly choke on my coffee.

"Excuse me?"

She waves her hand like it's the most obvious thing in the world. "You're basically family at this point."

Jaxon grins from across the table. "See? Told you she liked you."

"Jaxon," I warn.

"What?" he says innocently. "Mama's got a point."

Sadie leans in, eyes sparkling. "Y'all practically live together already."

"We most certainly do not," I snap.

The entire table bursts out laughing like I've told the best joke they've ever heard.

And Jaxon?
He just watches me with that lazy, heated look that makes my stomach twist.

Because he knows.

He knows I'm rattled.

And that I'm very, very close to losing control.

The First Real Slip

The problem with fake dating is that you have to sell it.

Constantly.

Which means touching.
Leaning in.
Smiling like you mean it.

And Jaxon?
He's very good at selling it.

Later that afternoon, we're at another staged event — a local charity livestock show. The cameras are rolling again, sponsors watching from behind makeshift barriers.

Jaxon leans in behind me as I review the event schedule, his breath hot against my ear.

"Smile," he whispers. "They're watching."

I force a tight grin.

He lets his lips barely brush the edge of my cheek.

A deliberate move.

Calculated.

Electric.

I glance at him sharply.

"That wasn't part of the plan."

"It's improv," he murmurs, his voice low and teasing.

I open my mouth to scold him, but the photographer snaps another shot before I can speak.

And the worst part?

It works.

The crowd coos. The sponsors smile.

We look like the perfect couple.

Later — Forced Proximity Intensifies

By the time the event wraps, a summer heat wave has rolled in — thick, sticky air pressing against my skin as we drive back toward the ranch.

Jaxon's old pickup rumbles down the dirt road, the windows rolled down, hot wind swirling around us.

"Successful day, boss," he says casually.

I glare at him. "You went off script."

"Relax." His grin is maddening. "They loved it."

"That's not the point."

"Isn't it?" His voice drops. "Or are you just mad because you liked it?"

I stiffen. "This is a job."

His eyes flick toward me briefly, heat simmering behind them. "Keep telling yourself that."

I stare out the window, trying to cool my racing pulse.

Because the worst part is…
He's right.

That Night — The Storm Breaks

The Texas sky turns violent fast — sheets of rain pounding the ranch house as lightning cracks overhead.

The power flickers and dies again, plunging the guesthouse into warm darkness.

I sit alone on the couch, staring at the flickering lantern.

And of course, he knocks.

"Power's out," he says softly as I open the door. "Again."

I stare at him, breath catching.

He's barefoot, wearing just worn jeans and a thin T-shirt that clings to his broad chest, damp from the rain.

I should say no.
I should send him back to the main house.

But I don't.

"Come in," I whisper.

He steps inside, closing the door behind him.

The storm howls outside, but inside it's... still.

Tense.

Electric.

We sit together on the couch, shoulder to shoulder beneath the blanket as thunder rumbles through the walls.

Neither of us speaks for a long time.

The air between us hums.

Every small movement — every accidental brush of skin — sends sparks dancing across my nerves.

Finally, his hand slides over mine under the blanket, his fingers warm, steady.

"Scarlett."

His voice is rough.
Soft.
Dangerous.

I don't pull away.

I turn toward him instead.

His eyes drop to my lips.
My heart pounds.

"You can't keep doing this," I whisper, my voice shaky.

"Doing what?"

"Pushing."

His voice drops lower. "And what happens when you stop pushing back?"

I can't answer.

Because I don't know.

Scarlett

The problem isn't the touching anymore.

It's how natural it's starting to feel.

His hand on my lower back.
His arm slipping easily around my waist.
The casual, intimate glances exchanged between staged photo ops.

They're all for show.

Except they're not.

Not anymore.

The Town Fair

Willow Creek's annual summer fair is exactly what you'd expect from a small Texas town.

Homemade pies.
Ferris wheel lights.
Livestock contests.
And a whole lot of gossip.

Jaxon and I are walking hand-in-hand through the midway, cameras snapping around us.

"This is PR gold," I murmur through my practiced smile.

"Admit it," he says, squeezing my hand. "You're starting to like small-town life."

"I'm starting to tolerate it."

He leans down, his lips nearly brushing my ear. "You like me."

"That's not the same thing."

"You keep telling yourself that."

I try to pull my hand away, but he holds on tighter, his smile wide and charming for the crowd.

"You're impossible," I hiss under my breath.

"And you're beautiful when you're mad."

The Ex Returns — Again

We don't get far before Lila materializes out of nowhere, like a viper coiled in designer boots.

"Well, if it isn't Willow Creek's favorite couple," she purrs.

I brace myself, slipping back into professional mode.

Jaxon's smile tightens. "Lila."

She turns her syrupy sweet attention to me. "You're glowing, Scarlett. Texas must agree with you."

"I adjust quickly."

She hums softly. "I do hope you're enjoying all this attention. Small towns don't always stay friendly when things get serious."

My jaw clenches.

Jaxon shifts slightly, angling himself in front of me, his voice calm but sharp. "Enough."

"Oh, don't be so touchy, Jax." Lila's voice drips with faux innocence. "I'm just making conversation."

"You're stirring trouble," he snaps. "Like you always do."

Her smile flickers, just for a moment.

Then she turns back to me with a smirk. "We'll see how long she lasts."

Before I can respond, Jaxon's hand drops from my back to my waist, pulling me snug against his side.

"She's staying," he says firmly. "Get used to it."

The way he says it sends a shiver straight through me.

Lila's mask cracks for just a second before she huffs and flounces away, her boots clicking sharply against the pavement.

Jaxon

I'm not usually a possessive man.

But every time Lila opens her mouth around Scarlett, something primal kicks in.

She's not just a job to me.

Not anymore.

She's mine.

And the more she tries to deny it, the harder it is to hold back.

Later — The Ferris Wheel

As if things aren't dangerous enough, the fair organizers decide a sunset ride on the Ferris wheel will make for perfect "candid" shots.

Of course they do.

We climb into the small gondola, the metal seat swaying as the wheel lifts us into the sky.

The town stretches below us in a glowing sea of lights.

For a moment, there's silence between us — the only sound the soft creak of the wheel and the distant buzz of the fair.

"You okay?" Jaxon asks quietly.

"I'm fine."

"You're stiff."

"I'm always stiff."

He chuckles softly. "Yeah, you are."

The gondola rocks gently again as we rise higher.

I turn toward him. "Stop it."

"Stop what?"

"Making this harder."

His eyes darken. "I'm not making this harder, Scarlett. You're doing that all on your own."

The wheel pauses at the very top, the entire town twinkling beneath us.

We sit frozen for a long moment — the tension between us thick and humming.

His gaze drops to my mouth.

My pulse spikes.

"Jaxon…"

His hand lifts, brushing a stray strand of hair from my cheek.

"You're scared," he whispers.

"Yes."

"So am I."

I hold his gaze, my throat tight.

We're dangerously close to crossing the line we keep dancing along.

His hand slides to the back of my neck, pulling me in slowly.

I feel his breath against my lips.

Just as I'm about to surrender, the wheel jolts back into motion, breaking the moment.

We both exhale, breathless.

Still teetering.

Still waiting to fall.

Scarlett

It's not *if* anymore.

It's *when.*

And I'm starting to think I won't have the strength to stop it.

Chapter 7: First Love Scene & Deepening Connection

Scarlett

Every second we've spent pretending has only made this harder.

The fake smiles.
The staged photos.
The polite hand-holding in front of cameras.

And all of it has led us right here.

To this moment.
Alone.
With no cameras.
No audience.
No distractions.

Just us.

The sponsor retreat is supposed to be simple — a quiet weekend at one of the ranch's private cabins, a carefully staged escape from the media noise.

But the second Wyatt drops us off with a knowing grin and drives away, I know exactly how dangerous this is.

Because we're truly alone.

No scripts.

No excuses.

No walls left to hide behind.

The cabin is small, but beautiful.

Rustic pinewood walls. A stone fireplace. One big bed in the center of the main room.

Of course.

I set my bag down, trying to keep my voice light. "Nice place. Very... cozy."

Jaxon steps inside behind me, his tone warm. "You nervous?"

"No."

He smirks. "Liar."

I turn sharply to face him. "We agreed to rules."

His smile softens slightly. "We're not breaking any yet."

"Yet."

The word hangs between us like a dare.

The Longest Day

The first few hours pass under a fragile, tense truce.

We review schedules. Organize talking points. Make calls to sponsors.

Professional. Controlled.

But the tension simmers like a pot about to boil over.

Every small glance.
Every accidental brush of fingers as we exchange papers.
Every polite "excuse me" when we cross paths in the small kitchen.

And as the sun dips low behind the hills, painting the windows in warm gold, the air between us grows heavier.

The Turning Point

After dinner, we settle by the fireplace, a bottle of wine open between us.

The flames cast soft shadows across his face, making his blue eyes seem impossibly sharp.

He watches me closely, like he's been waiting for this moment.

"Tell me something real, Scarlett," he says softly.

I glance away. "I tell you real things every day."

"No. You tell me controlled things. Managed things." His voice lowers. "I want something *real*."

I swallow hard. "You already know too much."

"Then tell me more."

The vulnerability in his voice disarms me. This isn't teasing. This is real.

I take a slow breath. "I was engaged once."

His brow lifts slightly.

"In New York," I continue. "He was perfect on paper. Smart. Successful. Polite. Everything my parents approved of."

"But?"

I force a bitter smile. "But he didn't want me. Not really. He wanted a version of me that fit his world. The polished, agreeable version. The version that wouldn't argue or challenge him."

Jaxon's gaze sharpens. "And you don't fit into neat boxes."

"No." My throat tightens. "And eventually, he decided I was too much trouble."

The words hang between us, heavier than I expected.

Jaxon shifts closer. "He was a damn fool."

I laugh softly, but it catches in my throat.

"You say that now," I whisper. "But people get tired of me."

He shakes his head. "You scare them."

I glance up, startled.

"Because you're strong. Smart. You don't take shit. And most people don't know what to do with that."

His hand lifts slowly, brushing my cheek with his knuckles. "But not me."

The air thickens again.

The fire pops softly in the background, but all I hear is my own heartbeat.

His voice drops to a near whisper. "You don't scare me, Scarlett."

My breath hitches.

"Jaxon—"

"Tell me to stop."

I can't.

I don't.

Scarlett

His hand is still on my cheek, warm and steady.

I should pull away.

I should remind him — and myself — why we can't cross this line.

But the truth?
That line disappeared a long time ago.

My pulse pounds as I lean into his touch.

His thumb brushes my lower lip, his eyes locked on mine like he's memorizing every inch of my face.

The space between us dissolves completely as he finally closes the gap.

His lips capture mine — soft at first, gentle.

Testing.

Then hungrier.

Deeper.

My hands slide into his hair instinctively as his arms pull me against him, his body hard and warm under my fingertips.

The kiss deepens quickly — no hesitation now — months of tension snapping like an overstretched rubber band.

He breaks away just long enough to murmur against my mouth, "I've wanted to do that since the second you stepped onto my porch."

I gasp softly, my fingers gripping the fabric of his shirt. "You're infuriating."

"You love it."

And God help me — I do.

The First Night

He lifts me easily into his arms, carrying me toward the bed.

The weight of what's happening sinks into my chest — heavy, terrifying, exhilarating.

He lays me down carefully, eyes never leaving mine.

There's nothing rushed about this.

No frantic tearing at clothes.
No reckless frenzy.

Just slow, deliberate worship.

His hands slide up my legs, inching beneath my dress as he kisses a slow path down my neck.

"You can still stop me," he whispers.

I meet his gaze, breathless. "Don't."

That one word breaks the final restraint.

He strips me bare with reverence, pausing to savor every new inch of exposed skin, his calloused hands rough but tender.

"You're so damn beautiful," he murmurs.

His mouth trails heat across my collarbone, my stomach, lower.

I arch into him, my breathing unsteady, my body burning.

He takes his time, like he's determined to memorize every sound I make, every gasp, every soft moan slipping from my lips as his mouth works me into a fever pitch.

When he finally joins his body with mine, the world tilts completely.

It's not just sex.

It's not just need.

It's *us* — raw, exposed, deeply connected in a way I've never allowed myself to be before.

Every movement feels like falling further.

Every kiss feels like surrender.

And when we finally crash over the edge together, I realize something terrifying.

I've never felt safer.

Because I trust him.
Fully.

Jaxon

I don't just want her body.

I want *her.*

Every complicated, brilliant, stubborn inch of her.

And now, finally, she's letting me in.

Her nails dig into my back as we move together in perfect rhythm, her breath soft and ragged against my ear.

I whisper her name over and over like a prayer.

When she finally shatters beneath me, calling my name, I follow her over the edge — completely lost in her.

And for the first time since my father's death, I feel whole.

Because it's her.

It's always been her.

The After

We lie tangled together beneath the soft sheets, the storm outside reduced to a gentle patter.

The world is quiet.
Peaceful.

Her head rests on my chest, one hand lazily tracing patterns along my stomach.

I stroke my fingers through her hair, holding her close.

For once, there's no teasing. No banter.

Just this fragile, dangerous honesty hanging between us.

Scarlett

I should feel scared.

Panicked.
Vulnerable.

Instead, I feel... safe.

Terrifyingly safe.

Because if I fall any deeper, I may not have the strength to walk away when this is all over.

I whisper softly against his skin. "This changes everything."

He tightens his arms around me.

"Good."

Chapter 8: New Scandal & The Push Away

Scarlett

I wake to the soft glow of dawn creeping through the cabin windows.

Jaxon's arm is draped across my waist, his breathing slow and even, his body warm against mine.

For a few stolen hours, everything feels perfect.

Untouched.
Safe.
Ours.

But perfect never lasts.

Not in my world.

By mid-morning, we're back at the ranch, smiling for yet another sponsor brunch, playing our roles like professionals — the golden cowboy and his polished city girl.

The sponsors eat it up.

But beneath the smiles, something is shifting.

I see it in Jaxon's eyes — the way his gaze lingers on me longer. The way his hand holds mine a little tighter when the cameras are rolling.

This isn't pretend anymore.

And that terrifies both of us.

The Call That Changes Everything

My phone buzzes in my pocket as we step off the stage after a perfect round of interviews.

I glance at the screen.
Adler.

I answer quickly, stepping away from the crowd.

"Adler?"

"Scarlett." His voice is clipped, urgent. "We have a problem."

My stomach drops.

"What kind of problem?"

"The worst kind."

He doesn't even wait for me to sit.

"There's drone footage."

I freeze. "Of what?"

"The cabin."

The blood drains from my face.

"Scarlett, someone leaked private drone footage of you and Jaxon. Kissing. Touching. In intimate positions."

My chest tightens. "How the hell did they even—"

"Doesn't matter," Adler snaps. "It's out. Spreading fast. The sponsors are panicking. The press is already running headlines about unethical PR manipulation. Conflict of interest. Professional misconduct. They're calling the entire relationship a staged PR stunt."

I press a hand to my forehead, nausea twisting in my stomach. "We can spin this."

"I'm not so sure this time."

"Adler—"

"The board wants you to distance yourself. Immediately. If this escalates, you're not just risking his career — you're risking yours."

I swallow hard.

"I'll handle it," I whisper.

"You'd better," he says sharply. "Because this could end both of you."

Jaxon

I see her face the second she walks back toward me.

Pale.

Tight.

Controlled.

The way she always gets when she's trying not to panic.

"What happened?" I ask quietly, pulling her aside.

She hesitates — just long enough for me to know it's bad.

"There's been a leak," she says finally. "Footage of us. From the cabin."

My jaw clenches.

"Footage?"

She nods. "Drone footage. Private. But it's everywhere now. The narrative's spiraling."

I exhale slowly, trying to stay calm. "We'll fix it."

She swallows, voice cracking slightly. "We might not be able to."

I step closer, lowering my voice. "We're in this together."

Her eyes fill, but she blinks it away fast. "You don't understand, Jaxon. My whole career—"

"I don't give a damn about your career right now."

"Well, I do!" she snaps, voice breaking. "Because this isn't just your life at risk anymore, it's mine too."

The words cut deeper than either of us expect.

The silence between us grows heavy.

"You knew the risks," I say softly.

"I knew the *professional* risks," she whispers. "I didn't know it would get this personal."

I reach for her instinctively, but she steps back.

"I need space," she says.

And the way she looks at me in that moment... it's like she's already slipping away.

Later That Night — Jaxon's Fear Takes Over

I sit alone on the porch long after everyone else has gone to bed.

The storm clouds roll in again, mirroring the weight pressing down on my chest.

I thought I could protect her.
Thought I could handle the heat.

But now?

Now I see the cracks.

The sponsors want distance.

Her job is on the line.

And I realize, for the first time, that maybe loving her means letting her go.

Even if it destroys me.

Scarlett

I've survived crises bigger than this.

Scandals.
Leaks.
Reputation implosions.

But this one feels different.
Because this time, my heart is tangled up in it.

And I don't know how to separate what's personal from what's professional anymore.

I sit at the small desk in the guesthouse, staring at my flight confirmation on the screen.

New York.

Back to my world.

Back to safety.

Adler's promotion offer still stands — a full partner track, corner office, prestige.

The future I always wanted.

The one I told myself was enough.

And yet…

The thought of leaving this ranch — *leaving him* — sends a hollow ache through my chest that no title could ever fill.

The Push

The knock on the door comes softly.

I know it's him before I even open it.

Jaxon stands there, his jaw tight, eyes guarded.

"You packed?" he asks quietly.

I nod. "My flight's tomorrow."

He swallows, his voice rough. "That's good."

The words slice right through me.

I cross my arms, trying to hold myself together. "You really want me to leave?"

His gaze flickers, just for a moment.

"This was never supposed to be permanent."

My throat tightens. "That's not what you said last week."

He shakes his head, stepping back like distance will make this easier. "You don't belong here, Scarlett."

"You don't get to decide that."

"I'm not going to be the reason you lose everything."

"You're not—"

He cuts me off, his voice sharper now. "You have a career. A future. I won't drag you down."

"You're not dragging me anywhere, Jaxon."

"You think this will work long-term?" he snaps. "You, living out here? Walking away from everything you built?"

The words hit harder than any scandal could.

Because part of me doesn't know how to answer.

And he sees that hesitation.

Seizes it.

"That's why you need to go."

The finality in his voice feels like a punch to the ribs.

I swallow hard, forcing my voice steady. "If you're trying to make this easier by being an ass — it's not working."

He exhales sharply, running a hand through his hair. "I'm trying to protect you."

"You don't get to make that decision for me."

The air between us crackles with everything we're both too scared to say out loud.

I step closer, lowering my voice. "You're not scared for *me*. You're scared for yourself."

He flinches — because it's true.

"You're terrified that if you let yourself want this, you might lose it."

His eyes shine, but he locks it all down. "Goodbye, Scarlett."

He turns and walks away before I can stop him.

Before I can fall apart completely.

Jaxon

I tell myself I'm doing the right thing.

Letting her go before I wreck both of us.

But watching her close that door?

It breaks something inside me I'm not sure I can fix.

The Family Intervention

The next morning, Mama corners me before sunrise.

Her voice is quiet but deadly sharp. "You're a damn fool."

"I know," I say flatly.

She sits beside me on the porch swing. "Then why are you letting her go?"

"I can't ask her to stay."

"Who said you have to ask? She was ready to stay, Jaxon. You pushed her away."

"I don't want to be the reason she sacrifices her career."

Mama sighs, gripping my hand. "Love isn't sacrifice. It's choosing someone, even when it's scary."

I stare out at the endless Texas sky, my chest hollow.

"You think she'll forgive me?" I whisper.

Mama smiles softly. "She already has. But you need to be man enough to fight for her."

I nod slowly, resolve hardening inside me.

No more running.

No more fear.

It's time to fight.

Scarlett

The taxi to the airport feels heavier with every passing mile.

My phone buzzes with updates from Adler, flight confirmations, client calls.

I should be relieved.

I should feel safe returning to the world I know.

But instead, I feel like I'm leaving the only place I've ever truly belonged.

And the only man who's ever truly *seen* me.

Chapter 9: The Grand Gesture

Scarlett

The city feels colder than I remember.

It's not the temperature — it's the emptiness.

The skyscrapers still shine. The coffee shops still buzz. The cabs still honk.
But none of it feels like home anymore.

Because my heart stayed behind in Texas.

I sit in Adler's office two days after landing back in New York.

The promotion contract sits on the sleek glass table between us, shiny and impressive.

Adler smiles as if everything is finally back under control.

"You made the right decision," he says smoothly. "This is where you belong, Scarlett. Power. Prestige. Security."

I nod automatically, but the words feel hollow.

Because none of it feels right anymore.

The Arrival

When the knock comes on my apartment door that night, I assume it's room service.

I don't expect him.

But there he is.

Jaxon.

Soaked from the cold rain, eyes wild and desperate, standing in my Manhattan doorway like a man who couldn't stand one more second apart.

My breath catches. "Jaxon—"

"I couldn't let you go," he says, his voice rough, breathless.

I stare at him, completely frozen.

"You were right," he continues. "I was scared. Of losing you. Of not being enough. Of you waking up one day and realizing this was never going to work."

He steps closer.

"But I'm more scared of a world where I never even tried."

My throat tightens.

"You belong wherever you want to belong, Scarlett. New York. Texas. Both. Neither. I don't care. I just want to be with you."

My heart pounds wildly.

"You flew all the way here?" I whisper.

"I'd fly across the damn world if that's what it takes."

The emotion in his voice cracks as he takes my hands in his.

"You saved my career. My family. My ranch. But more than that — you saved *me*. And I was too damn scared to admit it."

His voice drops to a near-whisper.

"I love you, Scarlett."

The tears spill freely now.

Because everything I've been holding inside finally bursts open.

"I love you too," I whisper, my voice breaking.

He lets out a breathless laugh, pulling me into his arms.

I melt against him as he holds me tight, his lips pressing into my hair, his voice thick with emotion. "Come home with me."

I pull back just enough to meet his gaze. "What about my career?"

"We'll figure it out. Remote work, split time, whatever it takes."

He cups my face gently. "I just need *you*."

The sob catches in my throat as I nod, laughing through my tears. "Okay."

"Yeah?"

"Yes."

The kiss that follows is nothing like the others.

It's not desperate. Not lust-fueled.

It's steady.
Full.
Safe.

It's *home*.

Scarlett

I was always chasing safety.

Structure.

Control.

Walls.

But real safety?

It's being held by someone who refuses to let you run anymore.

And I've never felt safer than I do in his arms.

Jaxon

I never cared about cameras before.

But today?

I care.

Because this time, I'm not hiding behind a PR spin or Scarlett's perfect talking points.

This time, I'm telling the truth.

We're back in Texas, standing in front of the media at the biggest press conference of my career.

The sponsors are here.

The investors.

The rodeo board.

Half the damn town.

Scarlett stands just offstage, her eyes locked on me, silently willing me forward.

And for once, I don't need a script.

I step up to the podium and grip the microphone.

"My name's been in a lot of headlines lately," I begin, my voice steady. "Some true. Some not so much."

A soft wave of laughter ripples through the crowd.

"But there's one thing I haven't said clearly enough."

I glance at Scarlett briefly, drawing strength from her.

"I made mistakes," I continue. "I lost my temper. I let my pride get the better of me. And I dragged people I care about into the fallout."

The reporters scribble furiously.

"But I also learned a hell of a lot this year."

I pause, making sure I meet every eye in the room.

"I learned that being a good cowboy isn't just about staying on the bull. It's about owning up to the times you get thrown off. And I got thrown hard."

More quiet nods. Cameras flash.

"I hurt my sponsors. I scared my team. I risked my family's legacy. And I risked the one thing that matters most to me now."

I turn fully, locking my gaze on Scarlett, my voice thick.

"Her."

The crowd holds its collective breath.

"Scarlett Monroe came here to fix my career. But she fixed *me*. She believed in me when I was too damn stubborn to believe in myself."

I let the words land.

"I'm not perfect. I'm going to make mistakes. But I promise this — I will own them. I will keep growing. And I will never take the people who stand by me for granted again."

The room stays frozen for a long heartbeat.

Then Mama starts clapping.

Sadie joins her.

Then Wyatt. Then Beau. Then the entire room erupts.

Reporters cheer. Sponsors nod. Flashbulbs pop like fireworks.

And for the first time in months, the weight lifts from my chest.

Scarlett

I've managed countless public statements in my career.

Crafted every word.
Controlled every narrative.
Anticipated every headline.

But none of them have ever landed like this.

Because this isn't spin.
It's not management.

It's truth.

It's *him*.

And watching Jaxon stand there — strong, vulnerable, fully himself — makes my chest ache in the best possible way.

Because I know:
We made it.

Together.

The After

As the press conference clears, he finds me backstage.

No cameras now.
No sponsors.
Just us.

"You were perfect," I whisper.

He shakes his head, pulling me into his arms. "I was honest."

"Even better."

He cups my face gently. "You really ready to stay?"

"Yes," I whisper. "I'm ready."

He leans in close, his voice rough. "Then let's start forever."

When he kisses me this time, there's no hesitation.

No pretending.

Just two people who finally stopped running.

Chapter 10: Epilogue & HEA

One Year Later

The Texas sunrise spills across the ranch as I rock gently on the front porch swing, a warm mug of coffee cradled in my hands.

The world is quiet except for the soft rustle of wind through the tall grass, the distant low of cattle, and the faint hum of Jaxon's off-key singing floating from inside the house.

A few years ago, this would've felt impossible.

Now?
It feels like home.

Scarlett

Life in Willow Creek isn't as fast as Manhattan.

There are no power lunches or skyscraper boardrooms here. No endless emails or cutthroat client meetings.

Instead, there's family.

Sunrises and starlit skies.
The smell of fresh-cut hay.
And the man who loves me without reservation.

I glance down at the tiny bundle nestled in my arms — our daughter, sleeping peacefully against my chest.

Tiny fingers.
Soft breaths.
Pure perfection.

I never knew peace could feel like this.

The Wedding

The wedding was everything the town hoped for — and nothing I ever imagined for myself.

It was loud.
Messy.
Perfectly imperfect.

The ceremony took place right here on the ranch beneath the old oak tree Jaxon's father planted decades ago.

Mama Hayes cried through the whole thing.
Sadie and Wyatt planned every detail like their lives depended on it.
Beau gave a shockingly emotional toast that had half the guests sniffling into their boots.

And Jaxon?

Jaxon looked at me like I was the only thing he'd ever wanted.

I wore white lace.

He wore a dark suit with his signature boots and bolo tie.

When he whispered "Finally mine" as he slipped the ring on my finger, my heart nearly burst.

The Adjustment

I still work, though not the way I used to.

Remote consulting. Selective clients.
Only the projects I choose.

Adler was surprisingly supportive of my decision to step back.

"You earned this," he told me with a rare smile. "And you were always a pain in my ass anyway."

It turns out, even power brokers in Manhattan respect the woman who can tame Jaxon Hayes.

Jaxon

She fits here like she was always meant to.

The way she balances her laptop on the porch swing while answering calls.
The way she learned to drive the old ranch truck with surprising speed — after a few near-death lessons.
The way our daughter clings to her like she's her entire world.

And she is.

Just like she's mine.

The Family

Mama still tries to pretend she isn't matchmaking every single person in town.

Sadie's pregnant again — "probably twins this time," according to Wyatt's pale face.

Beau's finally dating a local schoolteacher and pretending it's not serious, even though we all know better.

And the town?
The town has fully adopted Scarlett as their own.

Even Lila has found someone new to torture — thankfully, far away from me.

Scarlett

As the sun rises higher, Jaxon steps onto the porch, barefoot, shirt still half-buttoned, our daughter perched on his hip.

She giggles wildly as he bounces her gently.

"Morning, Mrs. Hayes," he drawls, leaning down to kiss me softly.

"Morning, Mr. Hayes."

He sits beside me, pulling me close, his free hand resting protectively over my stomach — where, in a few short months, we'll be welcoming baby number two.

I rest my head against his shoulder, closing my eyes as our daughter babbles happily between us.

This isn't the life I planned.

It's better.

Jaxon

Watching her here — barefoot on the porch swing, laughing with our daughter — still wrecks me.

Every single day.

Because there was a time I thought I'd never deserve this.

That I'd never be enough for someone like her.

But Scarlett Monroe didn't just choose me once.

She chooses me every single morning.

And I'll spend the rest of my life making damn sure she never regrets it.

That Night

After we finally settle the baby into her crib and tiptoe quietly out of the nursery, Scarlett turns to me in the hallway, that playful sparkle back in her eyes.

"We survived another bedtime routine."

"Barely," I grin.

"You look exhausted."

I step closer, lowering my voice. "I've got enough energy left for one more thing."

She arches a brow, trying to suppress her smile. "Oh really?"

I lean in, my lips brushing her ear. "Porch swing's looking pretty inviting."

Her breath catches. "That swing has a weight limit."

"Then we'll be careful."

Her soft laugh is the most addictive sound I've ever heard.

On the Porch Swing

The night air is warm as we settle onto the swing, the stars scattered wide across the inky Texas sky.

No cameras.
No scripts.
No pressure.

Just us.

She shifts, straddling my lap, her hands sliding into my hair as I pull her flush against me.

Even after everything — all the months together, the fights, the heartbreak, the reunion — she still takes my breath away.

Her lips find mine — soft at first, then hungrier, deeper.

My hands slide under her nightshirt, palms skimming up her bare thighs, memorizing every perfect inch of her all over again.

She gasps softly as I tease her skin, my voice low against her ear. "You sure you're not too tired, city girl?"

"Never."

Her nails dig into my shoulders as we fall into each other again — familiar, desperate, completely lost in this world we built together.

The creak of the swing rocks gently beneath us, a steady rhythm blending with our breathless gasps and whispered promises.

Scarlett

This ranch was supposed to be temporary.

Just another job.
Another assignment.
Another problem to fix.

But somewhere between the staged photo ops and the fake smiles, I fell in love with a man who was never part of the plan.

And now?

Now he's my home.

My forever.

As we finally collapse into bed hours later, tangled in each other, he whispers softly against my skin.

"Don't ever leave me again."

I smile, my heart full and aching all at once. "You're stuck with me, cowboy."

His arms tighten around me. "Good."

And with the soft Texas wind singing outside, I close my eyes — safe, whole, and completely his.

Forever.

THE END